Author's Note:

This story is based on "The Flea" in Ruth Sawyer's PICTURE Tales From Spain. I enjoyed taking an already ridiculous tale and stretching it a little further.

SQUASH IT!

Holiday House/New York

a true and ridiculous tale
adapted by ERIC A KIMMEL
illustrated by ROBERT RAYEVSKY

This story is true, believe it or not.

One day while sitting on his throne, the king of Spain felt an itch. He scratched beneath his crown and found a louse.

"Squash it!" his horrified courtiers cried.

"No," said the king, "this louse has bitten the king of Spain. It has royal blood in its veins. We must treat it with respect."

The king kept the louse in a jeweled snuffbox. Every day the royal rat catcher brought it a mouse to feed on. The louse began to grow. It grew until it was too big for the snuffbox. The king had to keep it in a chest. It fed every day on rats, then cats, and finally a mastiff from the royal kennels. The louse continued growing until it became so big the king had to keep it in a special stall in the royal stables. It fed every day on sheep and goats.

By now the louse was the size of a horse. It seemed friendly enough, so the king decided to try an experiment. He fitted the louse with a saddle and bridle and placed it in the hands of the royal riding master.

The louse proved to be a splendid pupil—quick to learn and eager to please. The royal riding master taught it how to trot, gallop, and canter. Soon the louse was tame enough for the king to ride. He rode the louse every afternoon at the royal riding academy. Of all the animals in his stables, the louse was his favorite.

One day the king arrived at the stables to find the
louse dead.

"It is Nature's way," the royal veterinarian
announced after examining the deceased. "Big or
small, lice seldom live more than a year."

There was nothing to do but haul away the car-
cass. First, however, the king summoned the royal
luthier, who crafted stringed instruments for the
palace orchestra, and asked him to secretly fash-
ion a souvenir of the king's pet. Using his utmost
skill, the royal luthier crafted a louse guitar. He
carved its body from the louse's shell. He fash-
ioned its neck from one of its legs, and from its gut
he made the strings. They vibrated with a deep,
mellow tone.

The louse guitar was a remarkable instrument. The king loved to play it above all others. One day it struck him that it might be amusing to see if anyone could discover the guitar's secret. First, he composed a song:

> I have a guitar. Hear how she sings
> With a heavenly voice when I pluck the strings.
> She's not made of wood, or metal, or leather,
> But something much finer, rarer, and better.
> What is she made of? Tell me its name

And you will marry a princess of Spain.

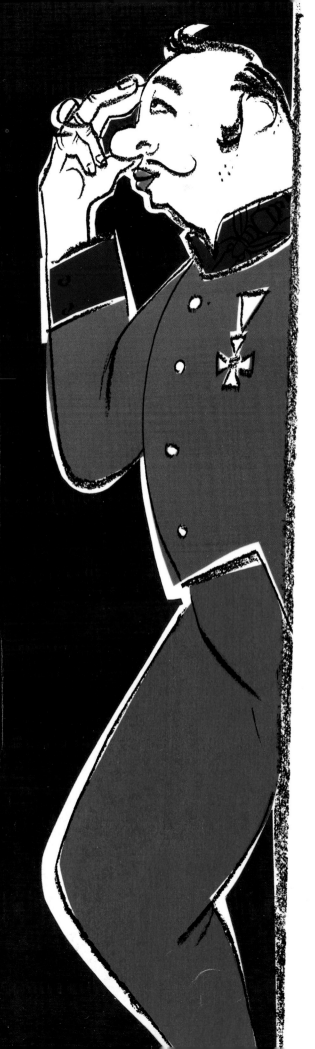

He sent a proclamation throughout the kingdom that anyone who could guess what the guitar was made of could marry the princess of his choice and acquire her dowry of wealth and lands.

Princes came from Germany, England, and France to guess the guitar's secret. "It's carved from alabaster," said one.

"A good guess, but wrong," said the king.

"It's made of Chinese porcelain," said another.

"Hardly," said the king.

"It's crafted from antique ivory," said a third.

"Clever, but incorrect," said the king.

Try as they might, no one could guess what the guitar was made of.

Now at this time, in the rugged mountains of northern Spain, a peasant lived with his wife and seven daughters. When news of the king's proclamation reached his village, the peasant said to his family, "Here's a chance to get something besides hard work and trouble in this world. I'm a good guesser. I'll go to Madrid and answer the king's riddle. We'll all be rich."

His wife and daughters began to weep.

"Woe to us!" they cried. "Father has ceased to love us. He will bring home a princess and we will be thrown out of doors to starve!"

"Silly chickens!" the peasant said. "Princesses are lazy creatures. They hardly do a pinch of work. Why would I turn out my good, strong wife and daughters for someone like that? On the other hand, if I could trade that princess for a good mule, there might be profit in that for all of us."

So saying, the peasant put on his wide-brimmed hat and traveling cloak and started down the road to the capital.

Along the way he came upon a grasshopper lying in the dust.

"Poor creature, are you ill?" the peasant asked.

"Ill I am not, but tired I am," the grasshopper sighed. "I am on my way to Madrid, but the road is longer than I thought."

"I'm going to Madrid. You can ride with me," the peasant said, setting the grasshopper on the brim of his hat.

"Muchas gracias," the grasshopper said. "I will return the favor one day."

The peasant continued walking. After a while he came upon a beetle lying beside the road.

"What's wrong with you?" the peasant asked.

"Alas!" the beetle sighed. "I am on my way to Madrid, but it is taking longer to get there than I thought."

"You can ride with me. The grasshopper will keep you company." The peasant picked up the beetle and set him on his hat beside the grasshopper.

"Muchas gracias," the beetle said. "I will return this favor one day."

The peasant continued on his way. After a while he
came upon a flea hopping up and down in the road.

"What is your trouble?" the peasant asked.

"My dog and I were going to Madrid to see the sights.
I fell off and got left behind," the flea answered.

"I am going to Madrid too," the peasant said. "There is
room on my hat. You can ride with us."

"*Muchas gracias,*" said the flea. "You are a true
gentleman."

"Let me try," said the beetle. He flew into the guitar and crawled around inside. After a while, he flew back.

"The king's right. It's not metal or leather. It isn't glass or any kind of pottery that I know of," the beetle told the peasant.

"I'll find out what it is," said the flea. He hopped onto the guitar and hopped back again.

"It's a louse," the flea said.

The beetle and grasshopper scoffed. "How can a tiny louse be made into a guitar?"

"I don't know," the flea replied. "But I've bitten every creature there is, and I can tell. It's a louse."

"Then I believe you," the peasant said. When his turn came, he told the king:

"Your guitar is made from a louse."

"You're right!" the king exclaimed, astonished that someone had finally solved the riddle. "And now you may choose one of my daughters to be your bride."

The three royal infantas of Spain came forward with great reluctance, for none wanted to marry a smelly old peasant with bugs on his hat.

The peasant stopped before each one and bowed.

"Don't pick me and I'll give you a rope of pearls," said the eldest.

"Don't pick me and I'll give you a sack of rubies," said the youngest.

"Don't pick me and I'll give you a chest of gold," said the one in the middle.

"Have you made your choice?" the king asked.

"I have," the peasant replied. "Your daughters are very beautiful, but since I am already married, I think it would be best for me to take a strong mule instead."

And so the peasant returned home with a rope of pearls, a sack of rubies, a chest of gold, and a fine mule to carry them. The beetle and the grasshopper went with him and lived long happy lives until a goat stepped on the beetle and a crow carried off the grasshopper.

The louse guitar was placed in a museum, where it can be seen to this day.

And what of the flea? By this time, he had acquired a taste for royal living, so he stayed behind at the palace, working his way up from page to count to duke to prince. Alas, ambition was his undoing! One day the king of Spain felt an itch. He reached into his royal robe and found the flea.

"Squash it!" his courtiers cried.

"Not so fast," the king said. "This flea has bitten the king of Spain. We must treat it with respect, since it now has royal blood."

The king wrapped the flea in a silk handkerchief and let it feed every day on one of his staghounds. The flea prospered under such fine care. It began to grow and grow until . . .

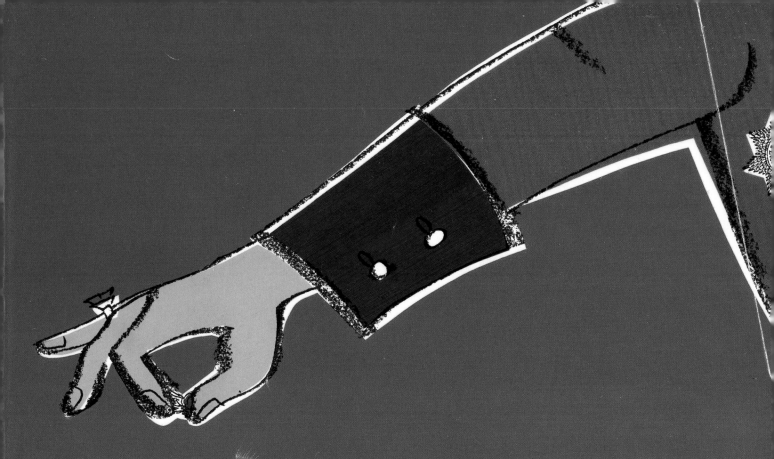

Ah, but that's another story.

To Matt
E. K.

To Bobra
R. R.

Text copyright © 1997 by Eric A. Kimmel
Illustrations copyright © 1997 by Robert Rayevsky
All rights reserved
Printed in the United States of America
First Edition
Book designed by Robert Rayevsky

Library of Congress Cataloging-in-Publication Data
Kimmel, Eric A.
Squash it / by Eric A. Kimmel ; illustrated by Robert Rayevsky.
p.   cm.
Summary: The king of Spain's fondness for a louse that bit him
leads to good fortune for a clever peasant.
ISBN 0-8234-1299-7 (Library)
[1. Folklore—Spain.]   I. Rayevsky, Robert, ill.   II. Title.
PZ8.1.K567Sq   1997   96-48128   CIP   AC
398.2′0946′02—dc21